A Little Christmas Magic

Winter Warmers Short Story Series

By

Suzanne Rogerson

Copyright © 2024 Suzanne Rogerson
All rights reserved. No reproduction without permission.

The right of Suzanne Rogerson to be identified as the author of this work has been asserted by her in accordance with the Copyright, Design and Patents Act 1988.

This is a work of fiction. Names, characters, places, and incidents are products of the author's imagination or are used fictitiously and are not to be construed as real. Any resemblance to actual events, locales, organisations, or persons, living or dead, is entirely coincidental.

ISBN 9798301433023

Table of Contents

Dedication
Poppy's Christmas Wish
Last Minute Dash
Driving Home for Christmas
The Honeymoon Period
A Christmas Toast
The Last Train Home
The Wrong Post
Looking After Belle
Dear Reader
Also by the author
Acknowledgements
About the Author and contact details

Dedication

I dedicate this book to Evie. She adopted us during the pandemic in 2020 and has been a part of the family ever since. But during the Christmas of 2023, she disappeared. Her story inspired 'Poppy's Christmas Wish'. I hope you enjoy it.

Poppy's Christmas Wish

Lauren stepped outside, her breath puffing out in a white cloud. She rubbed her hands together, trying to create warmth.

Her neighbour, Holly, was just squeezing the last suitcase into her Mini Cooper before slamming the boot shut.

'I hope you enjoy Prague.'

'I will. Darren's not so enthused about it, though.'

Lauren laughed as she adjusted her bobble hat. 'It's snowing in Europe right now.'

'That'll make the Christmas markets even more magical. They're not Darren's thing, so I'll have to ply him with plenty of local beer to stop him from moaning.'

Poppy burst out of the house, her coat buttoned up wrong and scarf dangling down by her knees.

'Come on, slowcoach. You'll be late for school,' Lauren said.

Her daughter pouted and slunk over, not her usual bubbly self at all.

'What's wrong, Pops?'

Please don't be coming down with something this close to Christmas.

'Kitty didn't come for breakfast.'

Lauren fixed the buttons on her daughter's coat and tucked in her scarf. 'Kitty's probably curled up asleep somewhere. Maybe her alarm clock didn't go off.'

Poppy shook her head. 'Don't be silly, Mummy.'

That told me, Lauren thought, as she shared a look with Holly. Not the best start to the day, being rebuked by a seven-year-old.

Waving to their neighbour, they set off for school.

'Do you remember what day it is?' Lauren asked as Poppy dragged her feet.

Her daughter shrugged.

'It's Christmas assembly. I'm coming to watch you sing.'

'Yes!'

Poppy's dour mood lifted. She skipped the rest of the way, singing a rendition of "We Wish You a Merry Christmas".

It was a shame Mike couldn't postpone his meeting to join them, but school assemblies were not his thing. Lauren secretly enjoyed all the festive gatherings. There was something so cherub-like about primary school children coming together to sing.

A thought niggled at her as she walked through the school gates - Kitty's crunchy bowl had been full this morning. It was unusual for the greedy cat not to show up and demand her breakfast before anyone else. Lauren tried to push the worry aside; it wasn't as if she could do anything about it now.

They stopped outside her daughter's classroom and she received a quick peck on the cheek.

'Sit near the front, Mummy, so I can see you,' Poppy instructed.

Lauren dutifully hurried through the playground and waited for the hall doors to open. She stood shivering along with the other mums, dads, and grandparents. When they were finally allowed into the building, she nabbed a spare seat at the end of the first row. There was the usual hubbub and chatter in the rapidly filling hall until the classes of excited pupils were led in by their teachers.

Lauren watched the children shuffle past. Some looked daunted, others excited, and a few almost tripped over as they looked for familiar faces in the crowd and waved manically when they spotted someone they knew. She had to smile. Christmas would be nothing without kids.

***

The house was quiet and no furry flash of white and black ran to greet her as she let herself in. The food bowl on the kitchen windowsill remained untouched.

Lauren checked under the beds and all of Kitty's favourite haunts, but there was no sign of her. She looked in the garden under all the bushes and shook the food box. 'Kitty. Where are you puss?' She called until the cold drove her back inside.

She had a few work calls to make, so it was lunchtime by the time she called her husband.

'What's up?'

'Can you remember when you last saw Kitty?'

Mike sounded distracted. 'Um, yesterday maybe. She ran out when I took Poppy to dance class after school.'

Lauren paced the kitchen, one eye on the window and the garden fences Kitty loved to patrol. 'I don't think she came home for dinner or her breakfast. What if something happened to her? Poppy will be devastated.'

'I'm sure she'll turn up. That cat likes her food too much.'

'I hope so.'

Lauren got back to work, but the feeling of unease remained. She checked the local Facebook groups for any news of cats being found. The posts were the usual complaints about potholes and the council's poor light display. Lauren hadn't noticed. She'd been too busy with work – she'd even had to do her Christmas shopping online this year. She used to enjoy the festive cheer in the high street shops, though not the miles of queues at the checkouts.

Lauren thought of her neighbours exploring Prague's fairytale Christmas markets. The retired couple were always jetting off somewhere. Whereas she and Mike hadn't been abroad since Poppy was born. Not that she'd change a thing…

She checked the clock. Damn. She'd be late for pick up. Poppy hated to be the last one to leave.

Throwing on her coat, Lauren had a last look around for Kitty and prayed she would show up soon.

***

Over the next two days, Lauren called the local vets and posted pictures online, asking for any sightings. No news was good news, Mike tried to tell her.

It was the last day of school and Poppy had been so busy with class parties, Christmas lunches and dance performances she'd barely had time to ask where her kitty cat was. At breakfast, she looked tired and forlorn and only picked at her food.

'I haven't seen Kitty for ages,' she said when Lauren asked what was wrong.

Lauren glanced at Mike, who sat at the table checking work emails.

'Cats are very independent creatures. They like to go exploring sometimes,' he said.

Their daughter's pout grew bigger. 'She will come back, won't she?'

'I'm sure she will.' Lauren jumped in. 'Try not to worry, Pops.'

'I don't want to go to school today.'

'But it's Mufti Day, and you wanted to wear your snowman jumper. And school finishes early for the end of term.'

'I'm too sad to have fun.'

Lauren shot Mike another imploring look. They'd talked about this, but she'd prayed Kitty would turn up before any serious conversations were necessary. 'When you get home, how about we put some posters up around the neighbourhood? Daddy can make them while you're at school.' Lauren slid the iPad in front of her daughter. 'Choose your favourite picture of Kitty while you finish your breakfast.'

Thirty minutes later, she'd dropped Poppy at school and let herself back in the front door. The Christmas lights flashed on the tree, barely visible through the decorations weighing down its branches. It didn't feel like Christmas was in just a few days. All the cheer had disappeared with Kitty.

'Maybe she found another home,' Mike said, guessing her thoughts.

She collapsed into the armchair where Kitty often spent the daylight hours sleeping. 'I can't see it, but it's better than the alternative.'

Lauren stuck on a cheesy Christmas movie and wrapped up presents while Mike worked on the poster.

When she was done, she hid the bags of presents in the cupboard under the stairs and then Mike handed her a bundle of freshly printed posters. She traced the distinctive black patches on the white cat. Kitty stared at the camera, the little smudge of black by her white nose in clear view, though it was her green, intelligent eyes that stood out most.

'I know it hurts, but we have to face the possibility she might not come back,' Mike said.

'Not yet. You hear stories all the time of cats coming home after weeks away. Kitty is tenacious. She'll be back.'

Mike cuddled her close. She rested her head against his shoulder, wishing for strength.

'Why don't I get Poppy from school? Then we can put these posters up after lunch.'

She nodded and blinked back tears as her gaze lingered on the empty windowsill. Kitty always sat outside, waiting to be let in. They joked she must have been royalty in a former life because using the cat flap was beneath her.

Lauren sighed heavily. She hoped nothing bad had happened to the little cat.

***

Poppy ran into the house, a wide grin highlighted by the chocolate smeared around her lips. She dumped her book bag by the door and launched herself at Lauren.

'Did you have a good day, Pops?' she asked once she'd drawn breath after the overenthusiastic cuddle.

'We coloured in pictures and read a Christmas story and had a quiz and a maths game. Then we had assembly and Mrs Lee was crying because she has to leave and have a baby. Alex asked if she was having baby Jesus.'

It was all delivered with such childlike innocence and Lauren had to hide a smile.

'Is Kitty home?'

'No, but Daddy got the posters ready, and I made your favourite tuna pasta for lunch. Go get changed and I'll dish you up a big bowl.'

'I want one as big as Daddy's!' her daughter insisted before she dashed away.

***

Christmas Eve arrived. They'd cleaned and tidied the house, ready to receive guests the following day. Lauren triple checked she had everything before the shops shut early and then Poppy helped her put all the presents around the tree. They put on Christmas songs and opened a tub of chocolates, but it still felt as if they were going through the motions.

Poppy was subdued as she sat and watched her favourite movie, The Grinch Who Stole Christmas.

After dinner, Mike came into the front room with their coats. 'Let's go for a drive and check out all the lights.'

Some people in the neighbourhood went all out with their light displays, while other houses remained dark and seemed to have an aura of sadness. It was sobering to remember that, for whatever reason, not everyone enjoyed the festivities.

Poppy oohed over the lights and bounced in her seat, excited to be allowed out so late on Christmas Eve.

Mike pulled up outside a very impressive light show. 'This place has my vote for the best display,' he said, turning around to look at them. Huddled up in the back seat together, Lauren and Poppy nodded agreement.

Poppy's eyes were wide as she took in the scene. Flashing reindeers fronted a life-size model of Father Christmas in his sleigh. A family of snowmen with light-up scarfs and bright carrot noses stood alongside penguins and polar bears. There were flashing lights in the trees and bushes, icicles hanging from the roof and windows and more light-up ornaments on the roof. *What must the electric bill be?*

'The man that lives here lost his wife a few years ago. Every year he adds a new light display in her memory.'

Lauren gulped, remembering the story from the local newspaper and Facebook.

'Where did she go?' Poppy asked.

'Up to heaven, sweetheart. Every year he raises money for a different charity so she will never be forgotten.' Mike held out a handful of coins. 'Shall we add our donation?'

'Yes, please.' Poppy unclipped her seatbelt and climbed into the front.

Together, they walked up the drive while Lauren watched from the car. Poppy fed the coins into a collection box and there was a QR code on the side, probably to a donation page.

She knew Mike was preparing Poppy for the worst, but she wished he'd discussed it first. Christmas was not the right time for a seven-year-old to learn such a hard life lesson.

'Okay, Pops?' she asked when they returned.

'I'm cold.' Her daughter climbed into her booster seat and clipped herself in.

Mike restarted the engine and turned up the heating before pulling away.

'How about hot chocolate and marshmallows before bed?'

'Yeah.'

'And we need to choose a snack and a drink for Father Christmas.'

'And his reindeer, Mummy.'

'Of course, we can't forget Rudolf.'

At home in the warm, the three of them put on their Christmas PJs and then made hot chocolate. Poppy added the mini marshmallows, counting out five for each of them.

After brushing her teeth, Poppy put out a glass of orange squash, a mince pie, and two carrots so Rudolf could share with his friends. Then she left a note addressed to Father Christmas in her neatest writing.

The last ritual was to put her present sack by the tree in the front room.

Lauren tucked her daughter up in bed and she was yawning and sleepy by the time they'd read a story together.

As Lauren came downstairs, she saw the headlights from next door's car. She hoped Holly and Darren had enjoyed their trip abroad. It had to have been better than her own last few days at home.

Remembering Poppy's note, Lauren detoured to the kitchen and picked up the letter, well versed in interpreting her daughter's grasp of the written word.

Dear Father Christmas

I am a very good girl but I don't need presents this year.

Please use your Christmas magic to find Kitty. I miss her.

Love
Poppy Jasmine Rogers
X

Lauren choked back a sob. Mike had read the note over her shoulder and put his arms around her. They didn't speak but made tea on autopilot, forgoing the usual bottle of wine and festive rom-com on the TV. Somehow, it didn't seem right to have fun when Kitty's fate was unknown.

'We need a little Christmas magic,' Lauren mused as she sat at the table and warmed her hands around her mug. 'It just doesn't feel like Christmas without her.'

'You'll be fine once the family gets here and we've opened our presents. And Poppy loves playing with her cousins. They'll cheer her up.'

'I suppose.'

While Mike checked on Poppy, she washed up and then gave the kitchen a last glance. At least everything was ready for tomorrow, even if she wasn't.

Mike crept downstairs and nodded that Poppy was fast asleep. Lauren kept watch at the foot of the stairs while Mike finished putting out the last special presents.

They were just about to go to bed when Lauren heard a sound - the cat flap banging shut.

She gasped and ran into the kitchen.

There sat Kitty.

She meowed rather hoarsely and walked towards them, rubbing and weaving between their legs. Her loud purr filled the stunned silence.

Lauren picked her up and held her close. 'Where have you been, little one?'

The cat rubbed her face against Lauren and then wriggled free. She went straight for her crunchy bowl on the windowsill.

'She feels so thin,' Lauren whispered as they watched the cat gobble down biscuits.

'This might be better if she's dehydrated.' Mike opened a pouch of wet food and swapped the bowls.

Kitty sunk her teeth into the food without complaint and it disappeared in seconds. Then she had another cuddle with Lauren, allowing Lauren to check her over for wounds or any signs of injury. Kitty's eyes were bright and she moved around with her usual lithe grace.

'She seems perfectly fine. Just hungry.'

Mike looked up from his phone. 'I've just googled what to do. It's best not to overfeed her. It might make her sick.'

The cat returned to her clean bowl and licked it hopefully. When no further food arrived, she sat and cleaned herself as if nothing had happened. Then she jumped down and weaved through their legs, meowing, before heading into the front room.

'Should we wake Poppy?' Lauren asked.

'Let's tell her in the morning, you know how manic Christmas Day is. We should get some sleep ourselves.'

Lauren sat with Kitty for a few minutes and stroked her. The cat prodded away on her blanket before curling up to go to sleep.

Lauren got into bed, smiling. It looked like it would be a good Christmas after all.

***

'Mummy. Daddy. It's Christmas!'

Poppy shouted, jumping on the bed between them. The rule was she wasn't allowed out of bed before seven on any day of the year, even Christmas. Lauren glimpsed the clock through hazy eyes just as the number changed to 7.01 a.m.

'Good morning, Poppy.' She hugged her daughter, breathing in the scent of strawberry shampoo.

The euphoric feeling from last night remained, especially after her first good sleep in almost a week.

Mike groaned and hid his head under the pillow. 'It's too early to get up,' he said, his voice muffled.

Poppy giggled and peeled the pillow away. 'Don't be a Grinch, Daddy.'

He grabbed her and tickled her until she squealed with laughter.

'Come on, let's check if Father Christmas has been,' Lauren said. She shared a look with Mike. Was Kitty still here or had she imagined her return?

Wrapped in dressing gowns, they headed for the front room. Poppy was ahead of them and burst into the room.

'Kitty!'

There, curled up next to Poppy's Christmas sack, was the cat.

'My Christmas wish came true!'

The cat stood and stretched and then butted her head against Poppy's hand. She purred loudly and her tail was up, even when an overzealous seven-year-old treated her to a cuddle.

Kitty led them into the kitchen, hopped up to the window and waited by her empty bowl.

'Can I feed her?'

'Of course, but I'll open the pouch.' Lauren did the honours before handing the food pouch to Poppy.

They watched the cat lap up her food. Only then did they see the untouched mince pie and carrots on the table.

'Father Christmas was too busy finding Kitty,' Poppy said knowingly.

'What about your presents? I'm sure I saw something in the front room for you.'

Poppy cheered and ran to check. She dived into the sack and pulled out the first present, ripping off the paper and shouting. 'This is the best Christmas ever!'

Lauren looked at Mike. 'I think you might be right.'

The house phone rang. She recognised the neighbour's number. 'Merry Christmas, Holly.'

'Merry Christmas. We saw the poster about Kitty.'

Lauren moved into the kitchen, where Kitty was cleaning herself in her usual spot by the window. She stroked her as she talked. 'Poppy wanted to post them through everyone's doors. But don't worry, Kitty came home safely last night.'

'That's the thing,' Holly said, sounding ill at ease. 'When we got back yesterday, Darren wanted to check on his precious plants in the greenhouse. He thought something ran past when he opened the door, and then he saw the damage to his planting beds. But it wasn't until this morning when we saw your poster that it all clicked together.'

'Oh my goodness,' Lauren put her hand over her mouth.

'That wasn't what Darren said with half his crop dug up, and you can imagine what else the poor cat had been doing in there. I'm so sorry. Is she okay?'

'Fine. A little thin, but at least the mystery is solved.'

Darren's greenhouse was built at the back of the garden, where it caught the best of the sunlight. No wonder they hadn't heard a response when they called for Kitty.

As if sensing she was the subject of the conversation, Kitty left the room.

'Poor little thing,' Holly said. 'I've warned Darren to check before he locks up. It gets so warm in there. You can't blame the creatures for being enticed inside for a nap while he potters about.'

'Tell Darren I'm sorry about his plants.'

'Serves him right.' Holly laughed. 'And there's a bonus - no greens for our Christmas dinner.'

Lauren said goodbye and returned to the front room. Poppy was wearing her new princess dressing up costume, while Mike had obviously been told to join in and had a sparkly plastic tiara perched on his head.

Poppy danced and waved a feathery wand, while Kitty sat on the back of the chair, watching the feathers dance. Her tail flicked as she poised to pounce.

Lauren grinned.

All was well in the Rogers' household. At least for now.

LAST MINUTE DASH

'Is there a problem?' The man behind me at the checkout asked as I stood torn between returning the box of novelty Christmas crackers or the tub of chocolates.

'Sorry, what?' I turned towards him.

He was young, early twenties, and dressed in very swish clothes for a last-minute dash to the supermarket on Christmas Eve. He wore a cream-coloured cashmere scarf and an expensive coat worn open over a dress suit, while I was wearing the same scarf and coat combo I'd used for the last three winters. Where he was all designer labels, I was charity shop chic.

'I meant, is everything okay?'

'Oh, sorry.' I flushed and turned even redder seeing his purchases on the conveyor belt - bottles of champagne and expensive boxes of chocolates. His dozen items probably cost the same as my entire shop for the month.

'I just need to return one thing and then I'm all done.'

It sounded so simple when I said it out loud, but I kept picturing little Kenny's face when there were no crackers to pull with our Christmas dinner, or shiny-wrapped chocolates to devour. I would normally stock up through December, but money was too tight this year after the rent increase and my hours being cut at work.

I turned back to the cashier. 'Take off the crackers... no wait, the chocolates...'

The young man tapped his foot. It didn't help my decision-making process.

I glanced at my trolley filled with yellow reduced stickers. Maybe there was something else I could put back instead. 'Sorry, my boy loves them both...' My words trailed off, no closer to a decision.

The manic atmosphere in the shop seemed to heighten around me. The festive music, staff rushing around wearing tinsel and Santa hats, all with excited expressions as they neared the end of their shifts with the promise of a well-earned day off. I had the overwhelming feeling that everyone was watching me, judging.

The man checked his watch.

I had to decide. Tears threatened as I double-checked my empty purse one last time. I was certain there was an extra £5 in there yesterday.

I sighed heavily, resigned. 'Take off the...'

The man behind me cleared his throat. 'Keep them both.'

'I can't...' How could I explain to someone like him that I was broke?

He stepped towards me and I flinched, not sure what he planned until he stretched over and tapped his card against the reader.

My whole shopping bill disappeared.

'But…' I floundered as the receipt printed off and the cashier handed it to me.

The man gathered up the notes and change I'd counted out by the till and pressed them into my hands. His impatient air was gone. 'Merry Christmas,' he said softly.

'I can't let you do that.'

'It's already done. Go and enjoy Christmas with your son.'

'You should at least take this.'

I offered him the money, but he shook his head.

'It's a gift.'

I bit my lip, looking down at the crumpled notes before stuffing them back into my purse. I quickly dumped the chocolates and crackers with the rest of the food in my trolley. 'Thank you,' I mumbled, not sure what else to say.

The cashier smiled at me. I could see his actions moved her, too.

As the cashier started scanning the man's items, I backed out of the way.

'Why did you do that?' I asked, watching him pack the bottles into a cardboard carrier.

He shrugged. 'I'm in a hurry and the self-service wasn't working.'

I nodded, not entirely convinced, but there was no point hanging around delaying him further. 'Well, thank you again. And have a lovely Christmas.'

I hurried away, my hands shaking as I gripped the trolley handle and wheeled it along with the other shoppers eager to get home and enjoy the rest of Christmas Eve.

He caught up with me as I neared the exit.

'That wasn't true, you know,' he said, falling into step beside me.

I turned to him, surprised. 'No?'

He smiled sheepishly. 'You reminded me of my mum, and of where I came from before all this...' He indicated his suit and the champagne bottles clunking in the carrier. 'We never had much growing up, but Mum always made Christmas special. Being a family was far more important to me than what we didn't have.'

My throat burned with emotion as I thought of Kenny waiting with his gran. 'I hope my boy is as kind as you when he grows up.'

He smiled and then strode ahead of me and out through the automatic doors into the darkness.

I hurried outside for one last glimpse of my saviour, but he was gone.

'Merry Christmas,' I whispered after him, before heading home to my son.

Driving Home for Christmas

'I can't believe you took an extra job on Christmas Eve. You promised you'd be done with the deliveries by midday.' Michelle's voice echoed in his ears as Nigel drove along the unfamiliar road, looking for the turn off.

She'd been so angry last night she'd threatened to make him sleep on the sofa, which was too small for his six-foot frame. It would have been a great start to a long shift behind the wheel.

He dropped his speed and scanned the roadside, left and right. 'Damn! Where the hell is the turning?'

He tapped the sat nav, but it had no signal. No signal bars on his phone either.

Nigel stared along the barrier of densely packed trees, but there was no sign of any houses. The clock on the dash was depressingly close to three p.m. It would be dark soon.

One last job to tag on the end of his shift, the boss had promised. A quick and easy drop off, just a bit of a drive to get there. He'd agreed to deliver the last-minute order to the reclusive millionaire's pad in the Oxfordshire countryside, as long as he got to spend the rest of Christmas with the wife and kids. He could see it now, tucking the boys up in bed and then getting back into Michelle's good books.

But this evening's plans relied on the delivery. And getting lost with one of the most important company commissions would not win him employee of the year.

The temperature in the van was dropping rapidly, forcing him to turn the heater up. Stranded out in the middle of nowhere, he'd be dead by morning. And if he wasn't, Michelle would kill him for spoiling Christmas.

He pulled over on a narrow verge to the side of the road and struggled into his company's maroon fleece jacket and the beanie Michelle bought him last year.

He let the engine idle as he consulted the map book kept in the driver's door. It was a couple of years out of date, but roads couldn't change that much, could they?

Nigel flicked through the pages and started from where he came off the M40 and travelled along the A44 in Oxfordshire. He traced the route all the way to his estimated location. It was just one long, winding road with no discernible links to residential properties.

According to the client's directions, he should have seen the turning miles back. Reclusive millionaire or not, he could have at least provided a phone number.

Huffing, Nigel turned around in the road, no mean feat in a Sprinter on the narrow country road that only accommodated two cars abreast. Not that he'd seen another car for miles.

He drove slowly and looked out for the turnoff, frustration building with every mile that ticked by.

Rob had said this last-minute order would ensure the business could open its doors on the 2nd of January. It was not just Nigel's future on the line if he couldn't get the package to its destination. He needed this job. He already worked weekends as a delivery driver and weekdays in the workshop building bespoke furniture. Anything to make ends meet. Especially now.

He pushed the thought aside and focused on the road. There were no streetlights, and he needed to find it before darkness fully descended.

A large deer burst out of the forest. Nigel skidded to a stop and watched the stag run across the road and disappear into the trees on the opposite side. A second deer crossed but stopped and looked directly at him, its wild eyes shining in the headlights. It was only when its pale rump had vanished in the undergrowth that Nigel let out his breath.

'Talk about strange,' he whispered to himself.

He set off again, warily watching the forest edge for more wildlife with a death wish.

The road seemed to stretch ahead of him, going nowhere as if it was being repeated in some spooky Groundhog Day Christmas nightmare.

The client had clearly stated the turning was off this road. He checked his phone signal again. If he found any bars, who would he call? The boss, or Michelle?

He'd promised when she'd waved him off in the predawn mist that he'd be home for dinner. She'd looked tired, but as beautiful as when they'd first met. Pregnancy always gave her a special glow.

The twins were nearly four now and excited about Christmas. They wanted him to help put out their stockings and read a bedtime story.

The clock hit three p.m. He had at least an hour's drive home once he found his way out of here.

Miraculously, a signal bar appeared on the phone. Nigel checked the mirrors and braked; he couldn't afford to lose this precious line of communication. The number dialled, and he prayed the signal held.

'Rob, I'm lost,' he said as soon as he heard his boss' nasal greeting. 'The directions don't make sense. Is this place even real?'

'The money in the bank account paying your wages is bloody real enough!'

'I've driven up and down this road and there's nothing but trees and freaking wildlife.'

'The directions are correct. I warned you this client is a recluse.'

As they spoke, the first flurry of snow landed on the windscreen. The soft flakes melted, but he could imagine his sons' excitement. They'd been asking about snow for weeks. 'It's getting late. I need to get home.'

'Just find it, Nigel. We can't afford to disappoint this customer. His connections could open doorways to a...'

The call cut off.

Nigel hit the steering wheel and started inching the van forward, hoping the mobile signal would return.

As he moved along at a snail's pace, he glanced at the trees and noticed light through the woods. How could he have missed that before?

The overgrown entrance wasn't signposted, but a small dirt track led to what looked like a small, solitary cottage.

It was the only sign of civilisation he'd seen for miles, not that he wanted to rock up to some stranger's door asking for help. He stopped and waited, checking the road in both directions.

A minute ticked by, then another.

'If you want to see your kids before their bedtime, just knock at the creepy house that appeared in the woods.' He laughed at himself. Great, he really was going mad.

Taking a last look in his rearview mirror and down the road, he indicated and pulled into the narrow lane. It was only wide enough to drive straight ahead and ended at the cottage.

'Let's hope someone's in, and that they're friendly,' he said aloud. Preferably with an intimate knowledge of the local roads and buildings, and not tourists on a Christmas getaway.

He rubbed his wedding band, thinking of Michelle. If these people didn't know, he might have to abandon the delivery. His marriage was more important than any job.

Nigel switched off the engine and walked the short distance to the cottage. Cold air enveloped him. He checked his phone hopefully, but it still registered no service. Stuffing it in the pocket of his jeans, he faced the cottage.

It looked normal enough, just small, and a little run down. Smoke rose from the chimney at the back of the house and a log store at the front was protected from the worst of the elements under a sagging awning.

He knocked and stood back, attempting to look non-threatening. Hopefully, the owners weren't the sort to chase off visitors with a gun.

A man opened the door. He was stooped with age, but his expression was still alert. Warmth and light flooded out around him as he waited for Nigel to speak.

Nigel offered him a smile. 'Sorry to disturb you. I'm lost.' He pointed at the big white van and flashed the map book. 'I've got no sat nav or mobile signal, but I'm hoping you can help.'

The man just stared at him.

Great! The only house for miles around and the old guy doesn't understand me. Nigel shifted from one foot to the other, wondering if he should cut his losses and leave.

'Betty, there's a young man here saying he's lost.' The man croaked out.

A woman, just as old, shuffled into view. 'You poor dear.'

She was small and dumpy, the opposite of the man's thin and hard angles. 'Fred, invite him in before he catches his death of cold.'

'I just need directions…'

'Nonsense. The water's just boiled.' She turned and disappeared inside.

Fred stood in the open doorway and shrugged. 'She won't listen. You may as well come in.'

Nigel hesitated on the threshold. They didn't look like murderers, but he'd seen enough horror movies to know not to trust first impressions.

The warmth was appealing after shivering outside in the snow. It was coming down more steadily now. If the temperatures continued to drop, it would be a white Christmas. The first his boys would experience.

He stamped his feet to stop his toes going numb.

'Straight through to the kitchen at the back,' Fred said.

Nigel walked to the kitchen and hovered in the doorway as he took in the old-world feel of the place. It had one of those iron range ovens, a chunky oak table in the centre of the room, an open fire and lots of exposed beams. Simple and cosy. Michelle had loved holidaying in places like this before the kids came along. Now it was all holiday camps with family friendly entertainment.

'Let's get you a nice cup of tea.' Betty poured tea from a teapot into a dainty cup. 'How do you take it?'

He was parched from driving all day and hated to seem rude. 'Just milk, please.'

Taking the cup she offered, he took a sip and sighed as the heat filled his mouth and warmed his insides. 'This is sorely needed. Thank you.'

'No trouble, dear. Now tell us where you need to get to.' Betty sat at the table and put on her glasses. Nigel took it as an invitation to join her and spread out the map book on the table.

'I'm looking for Lord Cranley's home. His estate is off the road somewhere around here, but so far, all I've seen is forest.'

'I haven't heard of a Lord Cranley or an estate by that name.' She squinted at the map for a few moments, her eyes magnified by the thick lens, though she still couldn't seem to focus.

'Fred will know. He worked in these forests for years before retiring. Fred?' she called. Without waiting to get a response, she waved her hand dismissively. 'He'll be here in a minute, no doubt. Now let's find something to go with that tea.' She groaned as she pushed herself to standing.

'Please, let me help,' Nigel was halfway out of his chair, but she tutted and pointed him back to his seat.

Betty hobbled over to a walk-in pantry in the corner. Inside, he glimpsed rows of shelves covered with glass jars and pots. She pulled a faded floral tin from the middle shelf and returned to the table.

She was still wrestling with the lid when Fred came into the kitchen. Snow was melting on his grey hair as he carried in an armload of chopped timber. 'Just topping up the supplies. That snow will settle, you mark my words.'

His wife poured him tea while he stacked the wood by the roaring fire.

'Have you heard of Lord Cranley? This lad's trying to get a delivery to his estate.'

Fred wiped his hands down his trousers and sat at the table. 'Never heard of him.'

He took a long look at Nigel's map, tracing the road and tapping a spot amidst the trees. It had no description at all, but a small nameless road led to it. 'You must mean the old Lannington place. No one's lived there for years. Run into the ground last I heard.'

'Lord Cranley has been renovating his property for some time, according to my boss. And it's very close to here, according to the directions I was given. I need to make this delivery today.'

He didn't mention the fate of the company was in the balance, or that his expanding family was desperate for him to keep his job. He was sure the nice old couple weren't interested in his woes.

Fred rubbed his chin as he ruminated on the information. 'Can't say I recall a sale to a Cranley, or otherwise. Tradition has always been to pass it down the generations, but Lady Lannington never had children.'

Betty patted her husband's hand. 'Times change, love. People move on.'

Nigel scrutinised the map again. 'It must be the same place.' He had to at least try, and if it wasn't, maybe someone there would know more, or would at least have a phone he could call Michelle on.

Betty finally succeeded in her mission to open the tin. As the lid came free, it released the mouthwatering scent of buttery pastry and sweet, spicy mincemeat.

'That smells delicious.'

Her eyes lit up at his reaction. 'I baked the batch just this morning.' She put one of the golden mince pies on a plate and handed it to him before topping up his tea.

Nigel's stomach rumbled as he took a bite; lunch seemed like hours ago. 'It tastes as delicious as it smells.'

'It's an old family recipe.' Betty beamed as she handed a plate to her husband.

Nigel scoured the map as he ate, becoming more certain they were talking about the same address. According to Fred, the Lannington place was rundown, and he'd been told by his boss that Lord Cranley was doing a full renovation. It couldn't be a coincidence.

Nigel finished his tea and let a minute pass before he stood. 'Thank you both for your hospitality. Now I really need to make this last delivery so I can get home to my boys.'

'We were never blessed with children,' Betty said. 'We had a good life here, though.' She smiled at her husband.

Fred nodded. 'Wouldn't trade it for the world.'

Nigel felt uncomfortable and looked away. Outside the cottage's small kitchen window, the snow was settling as Fred predicted. That was the last thing he needed; he couldn't afford to get snowed in.

Fred handed him back the map book. 'Reckon you must be right about the old place having new owners. I don't pay much mind to the goings on now I'm retired. Stuck in the past, aren't we love.'

'We certainly are.' Betty laughed.

Nigel glanced around discreetly. He couldn't see a TV or a single modern appliance. Not even an electric kettle. They used the old-fashioned type that heated on the stove.

'Hopefully it is the right place.' He tucked the map under his arm as Fred led him to the door.

'From here, turn right onto the main road and follow it for less than two miles. There's a turning, but it's discreet. A forked oak tree marks the spot.'

Betty hurried after them and handed him a mince pie on a linen napkin. 'Take this for the road.'

He nodded thanks before wrapping it up and tucking it in his pocket. It could be his reward once the damn delivery was out of the way.

The door opened and a blast of cold air seeped in. The snow flurry was increasing and a coating of snow covered the ground.

'Have a safe journey. Merry Christmas.' The couple called after him.

Nigel waved and crunched across the freshly fallen snow to his van. He switched on the engine and the headlights cut through the gloom of the woods around the cottage.

The old couple stood in the hazy glow of the open doorway and waved as he reversed slowly down the track.

On the main road, darkness was descending fast, but the route the old man had pointed out on the map was stuck in his mind. He slowed as he reached the part where he should see the turn off. Sure enough, there was the tree with the forked trunk and next to it, a small turning. Where had his head been earlier? Even obscured by snow and darkness, the road was obvious.

The narrow road wound through the woods, his sprinter taking up most of the track. There were several lay-bys, but thankfully he met no other traffic.

He drove slowly over the rutted ground, mindful of his precious cargo. Hopefully Rob had strapped down the furniture well.

He saw a glimpse of a building through a break in the trees. The grand house down in the valley looked straight out of a film. It was still a distance away, down a winding route that curved through the land and gave the occasional tantalising glimpse of his destination.

Eventually, he reached the approach road, which led to a long, gated drive. A fountain in front of the building pumped out water in a majestic arch. Lights captured the cascade, creating a moving tapestry made even more magical by the soft flurry of snowflakes. Michelle would have loved to see it, but he couldn't risk taking a photo and upsetting the client.

The gate opened before he could announce himself. He spotted the camera by the unmanned gatehouse and remembered seeing others in the trees along the route. Lord Cranley was clearly security conscious; no wonder Betty and Fred hadn't heard of him.

Nigel made the final ascent along the circular gravel drive and parked outside the double front door. The doors swung open and a smartly dressed, middle-aged man strode down the steps to meet him. Two muscular staff members who could have been bodyguards or bouncers followed him. Nigel gulped. Was it the right place? Or was he about to be given a beating?

'Lord Cranley?' he asked uncertainly. 'I have your delivery from Robert's Handmade Artisan Furniture.'

Lord Cranley looked at his watch. 'You're late.' He read Nigel's name badge. 'Not exactly Nigel Mansell, are you?'

'Sorry, I got lost. This is a tricky place to find.'

The man's stern expression relaxed into a smile. 'Exactly the reason I bought it. Now we need to hurry. My wife's helicopter is due in less than thirty minutes. I want this all installed in her study long before that.'

'I'll do my best,' Nigel promised.

Leather inlaid desks were the company's most expensive line. Especially when it was a rush job just before Christmas. The boss had worked the staff all hours to finish the client's specification.

Nigel hurried to the back of the van and unlocked the doors, followed by the bodyguards-cum-servants. With them breathing down his neck, it seemed to take forever to release the furniture from its strapping and manoeuvre it down the ramp. Pressure was building as the impatient customer paced before inspecting the work. At least the snow had stopped, but it was bitterly cold waiting out in the open.

Nigel waited for Lord Cranley's verdict, mentally crossing his fingers that everything was in order.

Lord Cranley rubbed his chin thoughtfully as he walked around the desk. 'I can see it's the right one, at least. I'll have to check it once we're inside in the light.'

Heavy and well-made, the company prided themselves on exceptional workmanship. Despite Nigel's protest, the men took over and carried the desk, one at each end. Nigel followed, carrying the matching chair.

They walked through an enormous entrance hall that was bigger than Nigel's house and along a double width corridor towards the back of the manor house. 'Lovely place,' Nigel couldn't help saying.

'We've just finished renovating,' the owner said over his shoulder. 'Five years, and this will be our first Christmas here. I want everything to be perfect.'

That's probably why the old couple hadn't heard of them, Nigel kept the thought to himself.

'The study is just through here.' Lord Cranley directed them through to an open room and pointed to the exact spot he wanted the desk. He stood back, firing orders to tweak the final positioning of the desk and chair.

Once he'd confirmed his satisfaction, Nigel removed the remaining protective packaging and tape holding the drawers closed. The man walked around the desk, running his hand along the smooth wood, which shone in the mood-lit study. The leather green top and gold fastenings finished the look perfectly.

Nigel felt a moment of pride seeing it in situ and smiled at the client. 'The boss oversaw the project himself. He ensured every last detail was finished to perfection.'

'I'm impressed. I think the wife will be even more so. She's always harped on about having a book inside her, so now she has the perfect space to set it free.' He waved his arms at the lavish space. 'Every piece of furniture, down to the tiniest piece of décor, has been selected to create a spectacular workspace for her.'

Nigel could picture a novelist holed up for days knocking out a manuscript. 'It's a beautiful room.'

'Only the best for my wife. Talking of which, she'll be back from the premiere any minute.' Lord Cranley ushered them from the study and locked the door behind them. Only then did Nigel see the big Christmas coloured ribbon and bow fixed to the door.

So, the entire room was a present – no wonder he'd been so desperate to get the furniture delivered on time.

The staff wandered off to complete other duties, while Cranley walked Nigel to the door. 'Thank you for getting it here safely. And thanks to Robert for working so tirelessly to finish on time. It is the pièce de résistance to my Christmas gift.'

'It was touch and go for a while,' Nigel admitted. 'And this place was impossible to find. Even the old couple down the road struggled to give me directions…'

Lord Cranley frowned. 'There is no couple down the road. That's the whole reason I spent millions on the place. Quiet, discreet, no neighbours in a five-mile radius.'

His 'best people' had clearly missed the friendly old couple. 'I was just at their cottage.'

'I don't think so. There's nothing but a derelict old worker's cottage on the edge of the woods and farmland.'

'These two wouldn't bother anyone.'

'Believe me, I had the location thoroughly researched before I made this purchase. Speaking of which, I take it I can rely on your discretion. I don't expect the paparazzi turning up at my door.'

'No, of course.' Nigel wondered who this man and his family were, and why they were so concerned with secrecy and security.

Lord Cranley shook his hand. 'Robert said you were his most trustworthy employee, and that you gave up spending Christmas Eve with your sons.

This is a small token of my appreciation.' He handed Nigel two fifty-pound notes. 'You can get them something special in the sales.'

'Thank you, Lord Cranley. I wasn't expecting anything.' He wasn't sure about accepting the money, but he had sacrificed precious time with the boys.

'I like to reward dedication like yours. The world wouldn't work without it.'

Nigel stuffed the money in his pocket before hurrying to his van and chucking the packaging in the back. Now he was ready to start Christmas. No work or deliveries for an entire week. Just Michelle and the twins.

He climbed in behind the wheel and started the engine. As he flicked on the radio, he caught the end of the song "Driving Home for Christmas".

Grinning to himself, he set off. The gates swung open as he drove towards them. Following the winding road up through the trees, he heard the whirring of a helicopter somewhere in the darkness.

That must be the wife arriving for Christmas. He guessed they were celebrities or something, but the name was unfamiliar. Michelle would laugh at his lack of celebrity knowledge. Another reason Rob probably chose him for the job.

He tried to focus on the road, but Lord Cranley's words kept coming back to him – no one lived in a five-mile radius. How could they have missed the little cottage?

At the end of the road, Nigel turned left instead of right. It was only two miles away. What was another slight delay to satisfy his curiosity?

It was fully dark, the road lit only by his headlights. On full beam, it picked out the shadows of snow-covered trees. He almost missed the turning again and would have driven straight past if he hadn't noticed muddy tyre tracks in the snow.

His van had churned up the narrow path. The cottage was no longer lit. Complete darkness greeted him.

Nigel parked up but left the engine running and the headlights on full-beam.

He used his phone torch and approached the cottage, his skin prickling with every step. Something was definitely not right.

No light, no smell of wood-smoke. The door was hanging from its hinges and the windows were boarded up. The awning was broken and hung down. There was one set of footprints in the snow, and he recognised the deep impression of his DMs.

'What the…' His words puffed out as clouds. The cold got inside his jacket, and he shivered as though the hand of death had just run up his spine.

Where the hell were Fred and Betty?

Nigel took a last look at the desolate cottage and then ran back to his van. He locked the door and reversed at speed out onto the road.

With the heater on full blast, he drove away, but he was still chilled to the bone by the time he turned off the M40 for the last leg of the journey home.

***

Nigel walked through the front door and was greeted by two excited boys dressed in matching dressing gowns and PJs. He hugged them tight, breathing in the scent of freshly washed hair. He wriggled out of his jacket and threw it on the sofa, stifling in the heat of the house after the freezing journey home. It had taken miles for the shivering to stop.

The boys filled him in on the things they'd done, speaking at a hundred miles an hour as they bounced around the room. A frazzled-looking Michelle showed they'd probably been hyper all day, and he felt bad that he'd left her to cope alone again.

'Sounds like you had a busy day,' Nigel said, ruffling identical blonde curls.

'We made cookies for Father Christmas.'

He laughed as they grabbed his hands and led him to the kitchen.

'And this one's for you.'

Michelle quietly watched them. When she caught his gaze, she mouthed, 'Are you okay?'

He nodded and made a show of sampling the cookie covered in bright green icing, silver edible balls and sprinkles. The overpowering sweetness was enough to make his teeth hurt, but he made appreciative sounds. 'Delicious. 10 out of 10.'

The boys cheered.

Michelle waved for them to calm down. 'It's bedtime, remember? I only let you stay up so you could say goodnight to Daddy.'

'Come on. Time for bed. Let Mummy rest.'

He tucked them up and read a few stories until they'd calmed down and looked ready to drop off to sleep.

Michelle was on the sofa with her legs curled beneath her while she watched TV. The news showed clips of a red-carpet celebrity premiere of some film or another. He dropped into the seat next to her and pulled her into his arms.

'You okay, babe?' she asked, snuggling against him.

'It was a long, strange day.'

'Long is the word.' She yawned and rubbed her back. 'Your dinner's in the oven.'

'Thanks, I'll get it in a minute. Just want to enjoy this moment.' He held her close, savouring her feel, her warmth, the solid baby bump – all reassuringly real.

Maybe the visit was a dream. Or a hallucination. The mind could play tricks if put under enough stress, and the last few months had been difficult trying to save enough to support their growing family.

'You made the delivery okay, then?'

'Eventually.' He told her about the lavish Cranley home and the client's paranoia. 'They must be rich and famous or something, but damned if I recognised him.' He remembered the tip and patted his jeans pocket.

'He gave me something. Look in the pocket.' He indicated for Michelle to check his jacket, which was still slung over the arm of the sofa.

She pulled out the two fifty-pound notes, her eyes lighting up. 'Wow.'

'He said I should give it to the boys.'

Michelle weighed the jacket, frowning as she checked the other pocket and pulled out something else.

Nigel felt cold looking at the linen wrapped mince pie. He took it from her and unwrapped it; the squashed pastry smelt very real. Proof that he wasn't going mad.

But what was worse?

He didn't know what he'd experienced, but Betty and Fred had been kind and helpful.

Sometimes you just had to accept the unexplained.

Not that he could confide in Michelle. She got spooked at Casper the Friendly Ghost.

'Nigel, you're acting really strangely tonight.'

'Sorry, love.' He refolded the napkin and put it on the arm of the sofa. 'I forgot it was in there. It's probably stale now.'

'I've never known you to forget about food or be so preoccupied.'

'I'm just glad to be home with you and the boys, and this little one.' He rested his hand on her belly and felt the baby kick.

'And we're glad to have you.' Michelle kissed his lips. 'Now stop fretting and relax. It's Christmas.'

Nigel smiled down at her and realised how lucky he was. He might not have the biggest house or be able to afford to chauffeur his wife around in helicopters, but tonight he felt the richest man alive.

The Honeymoon Period

Elowen hit the button on the alarm clock and groaned, before rolling over in the covers. The bed was empty beside her.

Stan arrived a minute later with a cup of tea. He perched on the edge of the bed and planted a kiss on her forehead. 'Merry Christmas, Mrs Shallon.'

She grinned; it still thrilled her hearing the name. 'Come back to bed.' She stroked the covers suggestively.

'Not if we're going to beat the holiday traffic.'

She pouted. He'd been so busy at work lately that she feared their newly wedded bliss was already wearing off.

Sighing in resignation, Elowen dressed and hurried downstairs for a quick breakfast, all the time being mindful not to wake her parents.

Regret pierced her as Stan packed their bags in the car and she faced her childhood home. She'd spent every one of her twenty-two Christmases in this house. But a new husband and a new life awaited - if only they could agree where to set up home together.

Stan started the engine of his beloved Ford Cortina and as they drove out of the cul-de-sac, the radio came to life.

'It's Christmas Eve folks, and here's the official 1975 Christmas number one... Bohemian Rhapsody.'

Stan grinned across at her as he cranked up the volume. 'Cornwall, here we come.'

***

'It's good to be back,' Elowen said as they pulled up in a parking bay outside The Ship Inn. Wintry clouds greeted them, but even a grey day couldn't dispel the warm glow inside her as she soaked in the view. Lowenporth was beautiful even without the colours of summer.

Stan had proposed here - on the golden sands of Kerensa Bay. They'd married a few months later and had lived with her parents ever since.

As she got out of the car, he slung his arm around her shoulders, pulling her close. 'I know it's not the most exotic destination for our belated honeymoon, but...'

'It's perfect,' Elowen said as she cuddled up to him. 'I wouldn't want to be anywhere else.'

'Let's stretch our legs and reacquaint ourselves with the town before checking into our room.' Stan locked the car and led her across the road to the beach.

Wrapped up snug in their winter coats, they strolled along the bay with the sea crashing dark and moody at their side. It seemed as if they were the only two people brave enough to battle the winter elements.

Elowen glanced at her husband; the tension from the long drive had already dropped from his face and he hummed a Christmas tune. Maybe he would be more like his old self now he could escape work for a few days.

'You look so at home here,' she said.

'Lowenporth is everything I've ever dreamt of, El.'

'I know. It's a magical little spot to set up home in.' She quoted his words back at him and squeezed his hand to show she was teasing.

The wind whipped his hair across his face. She stopped and reached up to tuck it behind his ear. A tiny ray of sunlight shone down from the grim sky and glinted on her wedding band. Like a sign from above, it provided her with the answer she'd always known from the moment they first arrived in Lowenporth. 'Okay, I'll do it.'

'Do what?'

'I'll move here with you.'

'But it's hundreds of miles from your family.'

'We talked about it when I told them we were coming to Cornwall for Christmas. They said it was my Cornish roots calling me back. They want us to go wherever makes us happy.' She spread her arms wide. 'And I think we will be happy here.'

'You really mean it? I would hate it if you felt forced into the move.'

'I love it here, too. The place makes my heart sing. It's where we're meant to be.'

He picked her up and spun her around, unfettered joy spilling from him. 'You're the best, El,'

After a long, passionate kiss, they turned to look up at the promenade where the old Victorian house sat an empty sentry over Kerensa Bay.

Butterflies formed in her stomach. 'Do you think the old place is still on the market?'

They'd both fallen in love with the run-down house that summer. It had been on sale for almost two years, "Waiting for the right owner", according to the estate agent. They'd viewed it on a whim during their holiday, but the madness of the wedding had taken over and she hadn't thought about it much since.

Elowen grabbed Stan's hand and they raced up the beach towards the house. The For Sale board was still visible outside as they clambered up the steps from the beach onto the promenade.

It was just as she remembered. The white paint was peeling and some of the lower windows were boarded up, but it still had a majestic charm.

The breath caught in her throat as the future Stan had talked about finally felt within their grasp. Then she spied the sign up close. The 'For Sale' board had a big red sticker across it.

SOLD.

'Oh, Stan I'm sorry.'

She knew how deflated he must feel. This was his dream, and her indecision had stolen it away from him. 'There'll be other properties in the area,' she offered half-heartedly.

He didn't take his eyes off the house.

'I'm so sorry,' she said again. How could it have turned from the best Christmas to the worst in a matter of minutes?

He pulled her in for a hug. 'Did you mean it when you said you wanted to move here?'

'Yes, of course. I'm as disappointed as you are to see the house already sold.'

She imagined the building after its renovation, and the excited guests arriving for their holidays. 'It was a wonderful dream while it lasted. I guess we weren't the right owners after all.'

Stan looked down at her with a familiar twinkle in his eye. 'Only we are.'

She frowned as he pressed a key into her hand. 'What's this?'

'An opportunity of a lifetime.'

He pulled her up the steps. 'Remember those work trips over the last few months? I've been meeting with the owner. I didn't want to say anything in case he turned me down, but he loved our vision for the place. He accepted my offer.'

She looked from the key to the view of the seaside town as Stan's words registered.

'I've only verbally agreed. My wife gets the final say.' He winked at her. 'The estate agent is meeting us here in an hour to get our decision.'

She couldn't find her voice.

'You need to be sure, El. It might be my dream, but it's going to involve a lot of hard work. Renovating and running a hotel is not for everyone…'

She put her finger over his lips. 'The answer is yes.'

Before he could offer her another chance to back out, she unlocked the front door.

'Wait!'

Stan swept her into his arms and carried her over the threshold. 'Welcome to our future hotel, Mrs Shallon.'

Elowen smiled up at him. 'What shall we call the place?'

'We'll think of something fitting while we make the renovations. Let's go with a seaside theme.'

Stan leant to kiss her before setting her back on her feet. She was so giddy with shock and excitement that she could barely stay upright. As her equilibrium reset, Elowen shut the old front door and propelled Stan towards the sweeping staircase. 'Let's explore before the estate agent gets here.'

'I have one more surprise first.' Stan's eyes twinkled as he detoured to the sitting room.

Set in the alcove was a small but beautiful Christmas tree decorated with tinsel and baubles. A golden, heart-shaped locket hung from its branches, and beneath the tree was a bottle of sparkling wine and two glasses.

She clutched a hand to her mouth, holding back surprised tears. 'How on earth did you pull this off?'

'I sweet-talked the owner. I told you how much he wanted us to have the place.'

'But what if I'd said no?'

'Well, I was really hoping you would agree. But if you hadn't, we'd have spent the holidays in the pub as planned while I secretly drowned my sorrows.'

Stan took the locket from the tree and she swept her long hair aside so he could fasten the clasp around her neck.

'You have left me with a problem.'

'What?' Concern creased his features.

'How will I ever get you a Christmas present to match all of this?' She waved to take in the building, the tree, the beautifully engraved heart around her neck.

He swallowed her in his arms. 'You gave me the best present of all when you agreed to be my wife.'

'Stan, you have such a romantic soul.' She planted a kiss on his lips and then broke away to reach for the wine. 'Let's toast our future at the new hotel.'

'Long may she reign over Lowenporth,' Stan said as he filled their glasses.

Elowen caught the view through the grubby bay window and imagined waking up to it each morning for the rest of her life.

Her parents had been right. Cornwall had been calling to her and now she'd found the perfect home and the perfect person to share it with.

(You can follow Elowen's story 45 years later in The Mermaid Hotel Series, as she continues to welcome guests to her majestic hotel. Series to be published in 2025.)

A Christmas Toast

They gather around the fire pit in the garden. Cathy, Harvey and Jane. My beautiful wife and children.

It's getting late, but I see every feature of their faces, how the firelight reflects in their eyes and their breath puffs out as they talk.

They pass a bottle of whisky between them, pouring shots into those fancy old crystal tumblers we only use at Christmas. The band of gold on the whisky label catches my eye - my preferred tipple. I can still feel the comforting burn of it slipping down my throat.

'This was his favourite spot. A little piece of heaven, he used to say,' Cathy says.

It's true.

I could while away hours pottering around the garden. There was always something to do - flowers to deadhead, weeds to clear, edges to keep pristine. I miss the sticky plant sap on my fingers, the unexpected stab of a thorn, and the dirt that stubbornly clings under my fingernails.

'Do you believe in heaven?' Harvey asks when several minutes pass.

They debate the subject as they shiver in their winter jackets and woolly hats.

I wish I could tell them. Maybe they would feel better if they knew death wasn't the end.

'Sometimes I feel as though he's still here, watching over us.' I hear the slight slur in Jane's voice and see the glisten of tears. Harvey slings an arm around his sister's shoulders but doesn't speak. If only I could comfort them like I did when they were young.

'I feel him too.' Cathy sniffs and sips her whisky thoughtfully. She stares into the distance. It feels as though she's looking right through me. It's heartbreaking being so close to my wife, knowing I'll never hold her again.

'I hope he isn't fretting over us. If there is something beyond this world, I want him to be happy,' she adds.

Oh Cathy. I gulp back emotion. Maybe it was a mistake to come tonight, but I couldn't resist being here for one last Christmas. It's always been our favourite time of year – all those silly traditions, too much food and good whisky, crap telly playing in the background while family games ensue. The usual arguments and making up.

'Charades isn't the same without Dad,' Jane says. 'He was always so bad at guessing the answers.'

Harvey laughs along with his sister. 'And acting out the clues always got more ridiculous the more he drank.'

'Remember that Christmas he got so into character, he fell into the Christmas tree and snapped it in half?'

They all laugh.

I remember it vividly, tripping over in those silly monster feet slippers the kids got me. I never lived it down. Not that I minded. Playing the fool was part of the fun.

They raise their glasses high.

'To John.'

'To Dad.'

I raise an imaginary glass alongside them.

To family.

Harvey adds another log to the fire before topping up their glasses. They huddle together and share their memories, laughing softly as they relive my crazier moments.

Their images begin to fade. I feel the pull to leave, but it's hard to let them go.

'Let them be, lad.'

I turn and see my father, just as I remember him.

'It's time for you to enjoy the afterlife.' Mum reaches out her hand to me and I take it. 'Everyone is waiting for you.'

The world of the living disappears. I guess it's time to make some new Christmas memories.

The Last Train Home

'Excuse me, Miss.'

Athena startled awake. She stared up at the guard standing next to her and then around the empty carriage. Where was she? What time was it?

'This is the end of the line, I'm afraid,' the guard continued.

She blinked rapidly, his words slowly registering. 'Oh, sorry.'

He had a kind smile. No doubt he dealt with people passed out drunk on the train all the time.

'Sorry,' she said again and quickly grabbed her bag.

'Was this your stop?'

'Um, no.' She wanted to run and hide with embarrassment. The last thing she needed was a fine. She fumbled in her coat pocket for the ticket.

The guard glanced at it. 'I'll overlook it just this once, but this was the last train. There's a cab office just outside the station. It's best to be safe at this time of night.'

'Okay, thanks.' She shuffled towards the door, not wanting to admit this wasn't the first time she'd fallen into drunken slumber on a train.

'Happy Christmas,' he called after her.

She stepped down onto the platform and looked around. All the other passengers had already departed. The station was cold, dark, and deserted, and the light from the train did little to dispel the shadows.

Her head banged with a pre-hangover. All she wanted was her bed.

She took a swig of water to chase away the sour mouth feeling before hurrying to the train station exit.

Another passenger was being escorted off the train. Highlighted in the glaring interior lights, she instantly recognised him. Hot Book Guy.

By the sounds of it, the guard was giving him directions to the same cab office.

Damnit!

Athena hurried away, not wanting to be seen with panda eyes and bed hair. She did what she could with her appearance as she headed for the portacabin office. Maybe she could sneak inside unseen and Hot Book Guy would find an alternative route home.

Acid rose in her throat, and she regretted the last glass of wine. If she was honest with herself, the last two were pushing it. But her work do's were always such a bore. Alcohol was the only thing that made them bearable.

The cab office was empty except for the controller working behind a locked section of the portacabin. She smiled warmly at Athena through the mesh window. 'Where to love?'

Athena gave her details and then sat in the sparse waiting area on a hard plastic chair by the heater. It gave out little more than a breath of warm air, but it beat the wintry conditions outside.

'Twenty-minute wait,' the lady confirmed.

'Thanks.'

She'd just finished texting her flatmate when the door opened and Hot Book Guy walked in, bringing with him a blast of arctic air.

'Another one fallen asleep on the train?' The controller asked, giving him a cheeky wink.

'I'm afraid so,' he laughed along.

'You're keeping us in business. Where to, my love?'

Anthea recognised the street name he recited as not being far away from her usual station.

'You're probably looking at a thirty-minute wait.'

'No problem.' He sat on the other side of the heater to Athena. 'Hi,' he said.

She nodded, her cheeks blazing with embarrassment. She felt like she needed to come up with a good excuse for being there. Not the truth. Anything but that.

'Good night out?' he asked, indicating the party frock hanging below the hem of her coat.

'Christmas office party. You?' She tried to guess by his outfit, but it was the usual jeans and duffel coat she regularly saw him wear on the train in the mornings.

'Nothing as much fun as you, just working late.'

'You haven't been to my work do's. I think I'd rather be working, or going to the dentist, or basically be anywhere else.'

'That doesn't sound good.'

She shrugged. 'Let's just say the job pays the bills. What about you? You seem to work long hours, and on the night before Christmas Eve, too. Your boss must be a real scrooge.'

'You could say that.' He smirked as he leant back and put his hands in his jeans pockets. She saw the edge of a paperback sticking out of his coat. She's never seen him without one.

'I run my own tech company up town. I'm working on a big coding project, and I made a breakthrough tonight.'

'You don't look like the typical techy geek.'

'Thanks, I think.'

With sandy blonde hair, a dimpled grin and intense blue eyes, he was even more ridiculously good looking up close than she'd expected. 'I see you on the train sometimes, but you've always got your head in a book.' She pointed to the offending item in his pocket.

He pulled it free and patted the tatty cover. 'Not just any book, it's a David Gemmell. He's one of my favourite authors.'

He offered it to her, and she read the back cover. 'I've never really read fantasy before. It sounds intriguing.'

'Gemmell was a master storyteller,' he said, as she flicked through the pages. 'You can borrow that if you like.'

She spotted the folded page of the dog-eared copy. 'But you're halfway through the story.'

'I've read it dozens of times.'

'Well, I do enjoy reading over the festive break while the rest of the family plays boring board games.'

'You can give it back next time you see me.'

'Thanks.' She tucked the book into her handbag. It was the perfect excuse to make contact again. 'It'll save me from monopoly.'

'Do people still play that?' he asked.

'God, yes. Every year, without fail.'

'I feel your pain.' They shared consoling smiles.

'I suppose you'll be coding over Christmas.'

'Actually, I've given myself the week off. Even tech geeks can have fun.'

She raised her eyebrows, making him laugh. The sound was warm and infectious; she could listen to it all night.

The taxi coordinator walked over and handed them both hot chocolates. 'Peace offering as there's still a wait on an available driver, I'm afraid.'

'Thanks,' they said in unison as she hurried back to her desk.

Athena heated her hands around the paper cup.

'I'm Elliot,' he said after a brief pause.

'Athena.'

'That's a beautiful name.' He blew on the drink and took a tentative sip. 'I look for you every morning. You always jump on the carriage closest to the station entrance because you're continually running late.'

'I'm surprised you notice anything other than your books.'

'I can't help but notice you.'

She swallowed her hot chocolate, rendered speechless.

'I've always wanted to say hello,' he continued, 'but I've never found the courage until now.'

'Then it's a good job we both fell asleep on the last train home, or we might never have spoken to each other.'

He nodded and stared into his steaming cup.

There was a moment of awkward silence, and she desperately searched for something to talk about. Her brain seemed to have deserted her, and Elliot didn't look inclined to say more, either.

'So, what does a tech geek do at Christmas?'

'The same as everyone else, I suppose.'

'Do you throw wild office parties, or make your staff sit in uptight restaurants over many tedious courses and hire DJ's that haven't updated their record collection since the 60s?'

'Now I see why you'd rather be working.'

She grinned. 'At least the wine's good.' *Too good*, she added to herself.

'Your driver's five minutes away,' the cab coordinator interrupted them.

Athena smiled her thanks. Then she swallowed down nerves with a mouthful of hot chocolate. 'You know, your place is on the way to mine. We could share... if you wanted to?'

Elliot shrugged. 'I wouldn't want you to feel uncomfortable.'

'It seems silly not to share when we're heading in the same direction.'

'Then I insist on paying for hijacking your ride.'

'That's not necessary.'

'I'll put it on company expenses. Make scrooge pay.'

They laughed and her stomach fizzed at the idea of spending more time with him, even if it was just for the short cab ride home.

Elliot confirmed the change with the controller. He lived in the nicer side of town, though it was only a ten-minute walk from her flat.

When their ride arrived, Elliot held open the door to the Prius and waited for Athena to get in before settling beside her. Sitting together on the backseat felt intimately close. It would have been comfortable enough if she wasn't battling wild thoughts of jumping on him. She'd often fantasised about doing more than just talking to Hot Book Guy, and now here he was in the flesh. It was probably for the best that she'd started sobering up, otherwise it's likely she would have made a real idiot of herself.

The driver put on some festive music and left them to chat as they set off.

'I have a confession to make,' Elliot said, looking awkward.

'Go on.'

'I didn't fall asleep on the train, I just pretended to.'

'Why?'

'When I saw you didn't get off at the usual stop, I wanted to make sure you were okay. I only intended to make sure you got a cab safely. I hadn't planned to spark up conversation.'

'You could have woken me on the train.'

'And look like a stalker?'

'I suppose it would have been weird. But it still seems like a coincidence us both being on the last train.'

'That was genuine. I was so caught up with work, I almost missed it completely.'

'You work too hard.'

'So everyone tells me.'

Conversation was easy between them again as they joked and shared anecdotes about their lives and Christmases gone by. It didn't feel like one-thirty in the morning; she could have chatted to him all night.

As they neared his stop, Elliot handed her a business card. 'You can use it as a bookmark, or you could call me if you get bored with monopoly.'

'I won't get bored now that I have a Gemmell book to read.'

'Then you must tell me what you think once you've finished it. I'd love to know if I've converted you.'

'I'll write a book report over the Christmas break.'

'In full essay form, I hope.'

'Yes, Sir.' She grinned at him.

Too soon, they pulled up outside his house.

'It was good to meet you at last, Elliot.'

'You too, Athena.' He reached for her hand and kissed it. 'Until we meet again.'

Elliot paid the driver and waved as they drove away.

'Generous guy,' the cabby said. 'He's a keeper.'

'I was thinking the same thing,' she murmured, playing with the business card in her hand. As the car turned down her road, she made a quick decision. She added the number to her phone and saved it as Hot Book Guy.

Fancy meeting for coffee and a mince pie in the morning? My treat.

A

His reply was instant.

I thought you'd never ask.

E

Athena held the phone to her chest. Despite the boring work party, it had turned out to be a fantastic night out, after all.

The Wrong Post

'Was that the post?' Kaz paused brushing her teeth to shout out to her husband.

He appeared in the bathroom doorway a minute later, sorting through a bundle of letters. None of the envelopes looked like they'd been through airmail from Australia.

'Sorry love. Just the usual, and another letter for number 39. I swear the postie's eyesight's going. It's the second time this week.'

Kaz swilled water around her teeth and tried to bury her disappointment. Their grandson's homemade Christmas card should have arrived days ago.

'It'll turn up. How about we drop this round to number 39 when we take Benji to the park?'

She poked Paul playfully in the ribs. 'You mean so you can nose at the new neighbour?'

'Well, it has sat empty for a long time. I'm hoping the new owner will sort out that overrun front garden.'

'Trust that to be your priority.' As a retired garden centre manager, Paul couldn't help noticing every blade of grass out of place on their road.

Putting on their coats and hats was the signal for Benji to run to the front door, his skinny legs shaking with excitement.

Kaz grabbed the formal-looking letter for the new owner at number 39, a Mrs N Raynord. 'Maybe they've got our Christmas card,' she said.

'You never know.' Paul clipped the lead on Benji's collar, who yipped and pawed at the door before yanking Paul down the drive.

Once Paul had the excited cavapoo under control, he linked his free arm through Kaz's. They strolled down the street past houses festooned with Christmas decorations and flashing lights which brightened the gloomy winter's day.

Paul looked up at the heavy grey clouds as they walked. 'Looks like snow.'

'I hope it settles, then we can video call the grandkids and show them. To think they've never experienced snow.'

'I'd rather swap places with them and be in the sun any day.'

'That's no fun.' She pulled her coat tighter around her. 'How can anyone enjoy Christmas in the middle of summer?'

'Maybe when you retire next year, we'll find out.'

She scowled at the thought of retirement. It was a sore subject between them. Paul wanted her to retire now, but Kaz refused to give in and admit she was getting old. 'So, if I retire, you're agreeing that we get to spend Christmas in Australia?' she challenged, knowing how much Paul hated flying.

'That's a maybe,' he said with a grin.

She rolled her eyes at him, before snuggling closer and enjoying the scratchy feel of his woollen coat on her cheek. The faint hint of wood-smoke clung to the fibres; the scent ingrained from the hours he spent with the small log burner in his workshop at the bottom of the garden.

'I'm looking forward to a lazy Christmas week with you,' he said, planting a kiss on her head. 'And when you retire, we can spend a lot more time together like this.'

'But retirement sounds so final. I don't want to be seen as past it.'

'I'm not suggesting you retire from the world, far from it. We can have lots of new adventures while we crack on with my bucket list.'

'Don't make me regret buying you that lifetime membership to the National Trust.'

'It was a wonderful, thoughtful gift. And it's inspired the perfect challenge.'

Paul had declared he would visit every National Trust property in England by the time he was seventy. They'd barely ticked off twenty this year, trying to fit it around her full-time job.

'I told you it was optimistic.'

'It doesn't have to be. You could retire tomorrow if you wanted. It's not like we're so desperate for money that you need to keep working.'

'Let's just get this letter delivered and pick up the discussion later.'

'Okay, sweetheart.'

That's what she loved about Paul; he never rushed her. As much as her reluctance impeded his plans, he accepted she wasn't ready.

What was so great about retirement, anyway? She loved her job, even if the other managers were half her age.

To distract herself from the thought of getting old, Kaz counted down the house numbers. 'I suppose 89 and 39 could be confused once, but we've never had a problem like this before.'

'I told you. That postie needs an eye test.'

Kaz laughed, feeling her tension ease. It was nice to have a relaxing stroll with the dog, rather than leave all the walking to Paul so she could get to the office early.

Benji took slow to the next level, though. He insisted on investigating every garden and peeing up every fence post they passed, despite his initial eagerness to fly out of the front door.

Eventually, they arrived at number 39. All the windows and the front door had been flung wide open, despite the temperature being below freezing outside.

'That's odd,' Kaz said. They'd seen the house moving trucks arrive a week ago, but no sign of anyone since.

'I'll knock and make sure everything's okay.' Paul swapped the dog lead for the letter, and Kaz hung back with Benji so as not to alarm the new neighbour with their over-friendly cavapoo.

As Paul rang the doorbell, a woman appeared wrapped up in a coat, scarf, and hat, so Kaz couldn't get a good look at her from the end of the drive.

'You're not the electrician, are you?' the woman said, looking him up and down.

'No, sorry to disappoint.' Paul held out the post. 'But I do come bearing gifts. We're from 89 and wondered if our post has been muddled with yours.'

'I'll have to check…' she looked around, flustered.

'Is everything alright?' Paul indicated the open windows.

'It's my own stupid fault. The electrics went this morning. No heating or hot water. I tried lighting a fire, but all the smoke backed into the house.'

'Probably a bird's nest blocking the chimney. Did you check the fuse box?'

'Yes…'

Their conversation fizzled out as Kaz watched the woman talk. The way she flung her arms as she talked seemed so familiar… but it couldn't be.

A tug on her arm drew her back to the present as Benji yanked the lead free. He dashed straight at the neighbour, avoiding Paul's attempt to catch him, and disappeared inside the house.

'I'm so sorry,' Kaz called.

The woman stepped aside for Paul to retrieve his dog, but her eyes were fixed on Kaz.

Kaz took a hesitant step. 'Nina?'

'Kaz?' Nina stripped off the hat and scarf, and it was as though she'd peeled back the veil of time to reveal her old best friend.

'It is you,' Kaz said, holding a hand to her chest. 'What are you doing here?'

'I just moved in.'

They both laughed at the obvious statement and then hugged as though the last 40-odd years hadn't happened.

'The name threw me, Mrs Raynord.'

'Not for long. I'm changing it back.' Nina tapped the envelope Paul had handed her. 'New house, new start.'

'I'm sorry it didn't work out.' Kaz saw her friend's unspoken pain and hugged her again as Paul returned with Benji.

He looked a little surprised to find apparent strangers hugging each other. 'This is Nina... my old school friend.'

He nodded hello, accepting the coincidence in his stride as he did with everything in life.

'I'd invite you in for tea, but there's no electric,' Nina said.

'I can check it while you two catch up.' Paul headed back inside with the dog.

'He seems very sweet.'

'He is. I met Paul at Uni and we got married as soon as we graduated. I sent an invitation to your parents' house.'

'I never got it. I went travelling straight out of college, met Denny, and got married. We never settled in one place for long. I lost track of all my belongings... and my friends...'

'How come you ended up back here?'

'I saw this place online, and it called to me. Now I know why.'

Kaz remembered how Nina had always been into psychic stuff. Maybe she'd been right to believe, after all.

'I plan to seize retirement and reinvent myself. Do all the things I missed out on while I was travelling.'

'Aren't you scared of, you know, getting old?'

'You just have to think about living in the moment, Kaz. Focus on enjoying what you have now.'

Nina's sentiment echoed everything Paul had been saying since he took early retirement. Maybe she was clinging to the past, too scared to let go of her youth.

Suddenly, the power came back on. The lights drew her attention to the stacks of boxes and piles of unopened post in the hallway. On top of one pile was an envelope to *Nanna and Granddad Willis*. The number was smudged, but the writing was unmistakable.

'That's us.'

Nina handed it over, smiling. 'I can't imagine you being a grandma.'

Kaz hugged the letter to her chest and mock glared at her old friend. 'I'm not, I'm Nanna.'

Nina grinned. 'Yes, you're much too grouchy to be a nice, cuddly grandma.'

'I used to think I was too young...' Kaz let the sentence trail off; with retirement looming, there was no way to pretend anymore.

'You'll always be young at heart.' Nina linked her arm through Kaz's. 'Come on, help me get these windows shut and then I can get the kettle on. We have a lot to talk about.'

Kaz followed her friend inside.

In the front room sat a huge, bare Christmas tree. There was nothing much else. Not even the TV was out of its box.

'I see you have your priorities right,' Paul said when he found them.

'I bought the biggest tree I could find. Just because I'm spending Christmas alone doesn't mean it can't be festive.'

'Good for you.' Paul nodded as he inspected the tree with a gardener's eye.

'And you don't have to be alone if you don't want to. Not now we're neighbours,' Kaz said.

Nina beamed, her eyes shining with tears. 'Thank you.'

Benji chose that moment to make his presence known by wagging circles around Nina and demanding attention.

As she fussed over the dog, Paul nodded at the open box of decorations and a tangle of Christmas lights heaped on top. 'It looks like we found you just in time.'

'I was supposed to make a start this morning…'

'Paul could lend a hand,' Kaz offered. 'He's a master at decorating a tree.'

'That's come from years of practice. I used to oversee all the festive displays at work.'

'Then please be my guest.' Nina waved at the box.

'Leave it to me.' Paul pulled up a Christmas playlist on his phone and then tackled the box of tinsel and baubles like a kid in a sweetshop. 'I'll have this done in no time.'

Kaz shared a look with Nina as they headed to the kitchen. There was nothing like reconnecting with old friends at Christmas. And suddenly the idea of retirement didn't sound so bad after all.

Taking Care of Belle

'Bloody dog!' Jack stared accusingly at the clock. It wasn't even six a.m.

The howling started up again, penetrating through the walls.

'For god's sake, Belle.'

He hid his head under the pillow, but the noise still reached him. He lay another minute listening, waiting for his neighbour to respond. It wasn't like Grace to leave her dog barking.

Knowing any hope of falling back to sleep was gone, Jack headed downstairs. He flicked on the kettle and called his neighbour's mobile to see if everything was alright.

There was no answer. By the time the kettle had boiled, Jack was already struggling into his coat and trainers.

Worry gnawed at him; Belle was usually a quiet dog, and Grace had always been a considerate owner. Could something be wrong?

Bundled up in his winter parka, he walked up his elderly neighbour's drive. The house was in darkness. He shivered, and not just from the cold, even though the wind blew straight through his thin pyjama bottoms.

He redialled Grace's mobile and could hear the faint sound of it ringing in the house before it went to answerphone.

At his knock, the howling stopped. Belle's blurry outline appeared at the glass door as she came to investigate.

'Hey, Belle.' He called through the letterbox, more confident with the glass panel separating them.

The dog sniffed at him and whimpered.

Jack tried to peer through the small gap but couldn't see much past the collie's fluffy mane.

Gus arrived next to her, meowing. The big Maine Coon looked up at the door as if expecting Jack to enter.

He put to his mouth to the letterbox. 'Grace? Is everything ok?'

While he waited for a response, the dog paced and the cat meowed.

'Grace, it's Jack from next door.'

They'd been neighbours for over half his life. Grace had always felt like a grandmother to him, though since she'd got the dog, they hadn't seen as much of each other as they used to.

What if she was in trouble?

He couldn't just turn away and leave his eighty-year-old neighbour to fend for herself.

Jack sighed heavily. 'I'm coming in to make sure you're okay,' he called through the letterbox again.

His frozen fingers fumbled opening the key safe by the door. He hoped the code was still the same as when he'd last fed Gus while Grace was on one of her Warner holidays. It had been a while since his cat sitting services had been needed. Belle's arrival had changed a lot of things, but as the dog made her lonely owner happy, he could forgive the intrusion.

Jack took a deep breath, mentally prepared himself to face the dog, and then let himself inside.

He stood by the door, unable to see or hear anything. Sweat built on his brow despite the cold, and he took a moment to control his panicked breathing.

The house felt eerily quiet as he switched on the hallway light. His limbs were stiff with tension, waiting for Belle to come running at him, but there was no sign of her.

'Grace?' he called. Her hearing was going and the last thing he wanted to do was give her a shock.

Belle came to the end of the hall and barked once at him, just like Lassie from the old TV show. Obediently, he followed.

Turning the corner, he found Grace sprawled on her back at the foot of the stairs. The stair lift was still at the top. Gus was sitting guard over his owner and nudged her hand with his head.

The touch elicited a moan.

'Grace.' Jack dropped to his knees beside her and took her hand. 'It's Jack.'

Her skin was cold, and she looked pale in the harsh hallway lighting.

'Grace, can you hear me?'

'Jack?' She looked confused as she blinked and tried to focus on his face. 'What are you doing here?'

'Belle was howling. I guessed something must be wrong.'

The dog lay next to her owner, head down on her paws, watching her mistress with concerned eyes. 'She's my good girl.' She tried to pat her dog and flinched as if in pain.

'Where does it hurt?'

Grace looked distracted by the question before she focused on his voice. 'My ankle.' She decided and reached towards her leg, but stopped, wincing.

'Help me up.'

'Maybe you shouldn't move just yet.'

'I can't stay on the floor. Where's Kate?'

'Your carer?'

'Kate will know what to do.'

'I think I should call an ambulance first. Just to be sure.' Jack grabbed his mobile from his pocket, but Grace gripped his arm with more strength than he'd expected.

'Call Kate, please.'

There was no arguing with that. So, Jack dutifully found Grace's phone where she'd left it in the front room and gave the carer a quick call.

Kate sounded wide awake and shocked to hear a man's voice calling from Grace's number. Jack quickly explained the situation before she panicked too much.

'She'll be here in ten minutes,' he reported to Grace. 'Now I'm calling you an ambulance, no argument.'

She nodded, the fight seeming to drain from her.

He tried to make Grace comfortable while he spoke to the 999 operator and was assured an ambulance would be dispatched as soon as one was available.

True to her word, the carer arrived a few minutes later and Jack was happy to step back and leave her in charge.

She crouched down next to Grace 'Dear me. What trouble have you got yourself into this time?'

'I needed some water, and I thought I could walk quicker than the stairlift.'

'Well, you know that's what it's there for. And I see you're not wearing your personal alarm again.'

'I don't usually need the damn thing,' Grace grumbled.

Kate patted her hand gently. 'At least Jack raised the alarm for you.'

'Belle is the real star,' Jack found himself saying, feeling a little less frosty towards the canine. He didn't like to think how long Grace would have lain there if the dog hadn't disturbed his sleep.

'Such a clever pup.' Kate ruffled the collie's fur affectionately. 'Help will be here soon, Grace,' Kate continued in a soothing voice.

Grace nodded.

The carer asked Grace all the right questions about any pain or discomfort, but also opted to keep her on the floor until the paramedics arrived. 'I'll prepare an overnight bag for you, just in case. And I'll ask a colleague to cover my morning clients so I can stay with you. Jack will look after you while I sort everything out.' She turned to him expectantly.

'Yes, of course.' He nodded. 'There's nothing to worry about, Grace,' he said, flashing a grateful smile at Kate before she disappeared upstairs.

After what seemed like hours, the professionals arrived.

'Maybe you could shut Belle and Gus in the kitchen before the paramedics come in?' Kate suggested.

Belle hadn't moved from her owner's side, and Gus had sat on the stairs watching the goings on with an air of indifference.

Jack fell into the role of assistant easily and herded the pets into the kitchen with offers of food. Feeding instructions were pinned to the fridge, and it didn't take long to prepare their breakfasts. He left them tucking in, but when Belle realised the ruse, she started whimpering and scratching at the closed kitchen door.

He was glad to have the barrier between them, not that Belle had shown the slightest interest in him.

Jack hung back and watched the paramedics work, in awe of their efficient manner and how they kept Grace calm.

'Any idea how long she'd been here?' they asked.

Jack stepped forward. 'The dog woke me before six o'clock, so probably not much more than an hour and a half.'

A few minutes later, one paramedic pulled Jack and Kate aside. 'We're going to take her to the hospital. She might have broken something in the fall and the shock is kicking in now.'

'Such a shame. And so close to Christmas too,' Kate said.

Jack nodded numbly, only just registering it was Christmas in a few days. Grace would want to be at home with her beloved pets. He silently prayed the fall was nothing serious and felt quite emotional watching the paramedics wheel Grace outside.

'Jack?' Grace's voice sounded thin and frail as she called to him from the back of the ambulance.

'Look after Belle and Gus for me. They like you.'

He opened his mouth to protest, but she gasped in pain.

The paramedic offered her gas and air, but she pushed it away impatiently. 'They need feeding twice a day, lots of grooming, and Belle needs her daily walk.'

'But I've got work, and I've never looked after a dog before.' He cringed at the obvious panic in his voice.

The anxiety on Grace's face overtook her pain, and her eyes welled with tears. 'Don't let them take my babies away. They're all I have.'

Jack could feel both Grace and Kate looking at him, waiting for his reply.

'Dogs are easy,' Kate said, using the same reassuring tone she'd used with Grace. It had a similar effect now, sneaking under his defences. Especially when coupled with that disarming smile. He didn't want to disappoint either of them.

'Fine, I'll take care of Gus and Belle.'

'You're a good boy.'

Boy! He'd be turning fifty next year.

Grace turned her calculating gaze on Kate next. 'Now you must give Jack some tips on looking after dogs when you let him know I'm okay.'

It was the carer's turn to be caught off guard. Jack hid a smirk before jumping to her rescue. 'I'm sure she doesn't have time for that, Grace. I'll call the hospital later to find out how you are.'

'No, I'll rest easier knowing you two are looking after my babies.' She glanced back at the house, where they could hear Belle's heartbreaking howl. 'They need you, Jack.'

Kate cleared her throat. 'I'll stop by after my afternoon rounds and give you an update.'

'So, it's settled,' Grace said. She closed her eyes, signalling the end of the conversation.

Jack shared a look with Kate and shrugged helplessly.

She patted his arm. 'It's a good thing you're doing.' Then she climbed into the back of the ambulance.

Her praise ignited a little glow inside him that pushed aside his trepidation. He waved them off in the ambulance before turning back to his neighbour's home.

He could still hear Belle's whimpers from the kitchen. Though he'd been able to overcome his fear of dogs in the panic of the moment, it didn't mean he was cured.

'What have I got myself into?'

He took a deep breath and prepared himself to find out.

***

During his lunch break, Jack let Belle out for a wee in Grace's garden. He watched her from the kitchen window while he made himself a cup of coffee. The big, fluffy dog was not the terror he'd first imagined. In fact, she'd acted indifferently towards him, pining for her owner too much to pay him much attention.

It was strange to be in his neighbour's home without her, but as the official dog sitter, he'd felt obliged to stay in Belle's home rather than disrupt her further. Plus, having a dog in his safe space didn't bear thinking about.

After the ambulance left, he'd popped home, dressed and grabbed his laptop. Now he was all set up at Grace's kitchen table and worked from there. The familiar routine helped settle his nerves at being in such close proximity to a canine.

The collie meandered around the garden, sniffing in the bushes and along the fence boundary. On her return, she checked the entire house for her owner. She whimpered when the search proved fruitless and retired pitifully to her bed by the radiator in the kitchen.

'She'll be back,' Jack said, though he felt little conviction. The paramedics had warned they wouldn't know the extent of Grace's injuries until she'd been x-rayed at the hospital. He remembered her heartbreaking plea to care for her pets and decided he should do a better job.

'Come on, Belle. Let's try you with some food again.' He threw away her dried up breakfast and tried a fresh serving. Belle turned her head away from the bowl and continued to sulk in bed.

Gus, on the other hand, turned up at the sound of food and waited expectantly for his second meal.

Jack fussed over him instead. 'No chance, buster. You can wait until dinnertime.'

The big Maine Coon showed his disgust by leaving through the cat flap.

Grinning, Jack looked at the kitchen clock. It was almost one p.m. 'One last meeting before I'm done for the year,' he told a disinterested Belle.

Once he'd explained the situation to his boss, he'd been granted short notice holiday leave. 'Take the rest of the year off and enjoy a long Christmas break, Jack. You deserve it.'

Not having had kids or any close family left, the festive holidays normally passed by like any other day. He used to have a sherry and a slice of Christmas cake with Grace, but even that had stopped because of the dog. He'd never admitted as much, but Grace knew.

It was silly to think how he'd let the fear rule his life. Belle was nothing like the dog that had bitten him. It was so long ago the scars on his arm had faded, but he'd carried the trauma of the attack around with him ever since.

He had time for a quick lunch before his meeting and grabbed the sandwich he'd made at home. As he ate, a wet nose appeared on his lap, and soulful brown eyes watched him as he chewed.

He smiled through a mouthful of chicken and lettuce, not even tempted to chuck the sandwich and run to safety. The progress made him feel bolder.

'Fine, we'll share just this once,' he said, pulling out a chunk of meat for her.

Belle took the offered chicken gently from his fingers and swallowed it down.

Helping Jack polish off his sandwich restored Belle's appetite and he finally got her to eat the bowl of dog food. Then she curled up in her bed and had a nap while he logged onto his last meeting.

An hour later, Jack set out with Belle, holding tight to the lead for fear of losing her. He'd decided a circuit around the block was safest for his first attempt at dog walking. And even though Belle was helping with his phobia, he wasn't ready to face a park full of playful mutts.

The winter weather was biting but, wrapped up in scarf and hat, Jack felt refreshed being away from his computer screen.

He paused at the top of his road and sucked in a lungful of bracing winter air. It was a novelty to be out in the world rather than watching the days pass by through his window. Sometimes in the wintertime, he barely saw the sun. The days started with online meetings and by the time he closed his laptop, it was already dark.

The tree-lined street had a festive feel. Tall conifers were festooned with lights that were just coming to life in the growing darkness. Many of the houses he passed had some display of the seasonal holiday, making him feel a bit like a scrooge with his own home bearing no hint of Christmas. He didn't hate this time of year, but he hadn't had a reason to celebrate it in a very long time.

Belle walked sedately at his side; Jack supposed that was the perk of her having an elderly owner. The dog enjoyed sniffing around the neighbourhood and was a model dog for a nervous human. But once she recognised the route home, the collie dragged him back to her front door.

He was eager to be home, too. Hopefully, Kate would stop by soon with news of Grace. They should have swapped numbers, but that morning had been a blur, with no time to focus on practical matters beyond keeping his neighbour calm.

It was after seven p.m. when he finally heard a knock at Grace's front door.

He rushed to answer, hoping to see his sweet old neighbour returning home, but it was only Kate huddled in her coat and blinking in the harsh glow of the hall light.

'Hi,' he said.

'Sorry, it's later than I planned. My shift ran over, and then it took me a while to see how Grace was doing. Gosh, that lady can talk.'

They laughed good-naturedly. Grace had always been a chatterbox.

'I assume she's not coming home tonight, then?'

Kate shook her head regretfully. 'It doesn't look as if she's fractured any bones, which is a godsend. But her ankle's swollen, so they're going to monitor her.'

A gust of wintery air blustered around them, and Kate shivered into her coat.

'Sorry, where are my manners? Please, come in out of the cold.' It felt odd to invite a stranger into someone else's home, though he knew Kate had been Grace's carer for several years. They'd just never crossed paths before.

He led her through to the front room where he'd temporarily locked Belle.

As soon as the door opened, the dog launched herself at Kate, who talked and cooed at the dog in a way that came so easily to some people.

As they sat opposite each other, Jack in the armchair and Kate on the sofa, Belle lay on her belly between them, her head resting on her paws. She looked up forlornly, as if to say. 'What have you done with my Grace?'

'She's been like that all day.' He sighed, wishing he could do more to help.

'They dote on each other. And Gus too,' Kate said, looking at the Maine Coon curled up in the other armchair. 'Grace kept asking about them. I promised I would make sure you were okay looking after them.'

'It's been no trouble,' he found himself saying and meaning it.

'She did say you weren't too keen on dogs but that you'd looked after Gus plenty of times.'

He was glad Grace hadn't gone into too much detail. 'Belle's actually okay.' He reached over to pat her fluffy back, and she gave a small wag in response.

'I'm more of a dog person,' Kate admitted. 'Though it's hard not to love Gus, he's such a big softie.'

'Do you think they will discharge her soon?'

'Once she's mobile, yes. But because she lives alone, they can't send her home until she can take care of herself.'

'Grace has always been fiercely independent.' Jack thought about Grace stuck in a strange place, away from her beloved pets. She would hate it.

'Unfortunately, I see it all the time in my job. She was lucky Belle raised the alarm and that you summoned help. Not everyone is blessed with a caring neighbour.' She looked down at the dog sprawled between them and then up at Jack.

He smiled shyly when their eyes met, noticing for the first time flecks of green in Kate's warm brown eyes.

'Would you like a drink? Tea, coffee, sherry? It's Grace's favourite tipple at Christmas. I buy her a bottle every year.'

Kate looked regretfully at her watch. 'I should get back for dinner. Not that a ready meal for one is much to look forward to.'

'Would you like to stay here and call for a takeaway or something?' He looked away, embarrassed, not sure where the idea had come from. 'I could do with advice on how to deal with Belle until Grace gets home,' he added quickly.

Kate looked at Belle and Gus as the pets relaxed in the room with them. 'I think you're doing just fine, but a takeaway would be nice. I don't get to treat myself very often, not now I'm on my own.'

'Same,' Jack agreed. 'The local restaurant does a mean takeaway Jalfrezi, if that's your thing.'

'Curry would be good.'

Jack ordered for them on his phone app and then they chatted over a glass of sherry while they waited for the food to arrive. Kate was easy to talk to, and they found they were of a similar age and had a lot in common. Divorced, lived alone, workaholics…

When she eventually rose to leave, he swallowed back nerves. 'Maybe you'd like to meet up here again tomorrow, see how my first night as a dog sitter went?'

'Okay. I'll bring the food this time.'

Jack waved her off, feeling a lot lighter of spirit than he had in a long time. Just talking to another human being about something other than work had been a pleasure.

He grabbed some blankets and a pillow from home and made himself a makeshift bed on the sofa in Grace's front room. He placed Belle's bed on the floor nearby, determined to get a better night's sleep after his premature wake-up call that morning.

After a quick wee, the dog did another search of the house, before she settled in her bed with a loud huff.

'She'll be back before you know it,' he promised. He reached out in the darkness to stroke Belle and fell asleep with his hand resting on her back.

***

In the morning, Jack woke with a heavy weight across his chest. Gus butted his chin and purred loudly. Jack had to laugh as the huge furry head came in for another affectionate headbutt. 'I guess it's breakfast time.'

The animals rushed to the kitchen ahead of him. He let Belle out for her toilet and clicked on the kettle.

He laughed as Gus tried to get the food before he'd even emptied the pouch onto the plate and ended up getting gravy in his whiskers. 'Still the same greedy guts,' he said.

Once they'd all been fed, Jack wrapped up and took Belle for another walk around the block.

She was as well behaved as yesterday, and he felt confident enough to extend their walk to include a part of the town he'd never bothered exploring before.

An hour later, he let himself into Grace's home. It was cheerless compared to the rest of the neighbourhood. She always used to make a big deal of Christmas, but without his help, that had obviously become more difficult.

An idea formed as he made himself a hot chocolate and then sat at the kitchen table to text his thoughts to Kate.

She arrived after her shift ended at five p.m. with a bottle of red wine and two readymade beef casseroles.

He put them in the oven and set the timer.

'Come on, let's get to work,' she said, rolling up her sleeves.

While Kate cleared a space in the living room, Jack hunted in the cupboard under the stairs. Belle trailed after him as he pulled out the old cardboard box of decorations and the six-foot artificial tree Grace had used for the last twenty years.

They put up the tree in the living room, complete with lights, tinsel, and baubles in festive golds and reds. Then they sat and ate their casseroles while drinking red wine with the flashing Christmas lights and listening to festive songs playing quietly in the background.

After the food, Jack relaxed back in the chair with Gus on his lap, while Belle had taken a seat next to Kate on the sofa.

He sighed happily. 'This is the most Christmassy I've felt in a very long time.'

Kate seemed to glow in the tree's light. 'Me too.'

They leant towards each other and chinked glasses. 'We've made a good team,' Kate said.

Too soon, Kate helped him with the washing up and then reached for her coat.

'Can we walk you home?' Jack asked. Belle's ears perked up at the word.

'You don't have to. It's not far.'

'That's okay. We could both do with a walk, couldn't we, Belle?'

The dog looked at him, tilting her head questioningly to the side.

A few minutes later, they were strolling along, chatting like old friends. The world felt crisp and cold, but he felt warmed by the wine and Kate's company.

'So, what will you being doing at Christmas this year?' he asked.

'Working the morning shift and then the rest of the day is my own.'

'That's a shame.'

'Not at all. I love greeting my clients on Christmas morning. It's always filled with laughs, Christmas cookies and chocolates.'

'I'm sure you bring lots of joy to their days,' Jack said, while thinking of his own lonely Christmases.

'It's nice to give them company, especially when they don't have family around. Grace should be home tomorrow, too. At least it sounded promising when I called the hospital earlier.'

'We hope so, don't we, Belle?' The dog was too busy examining a tree trunk to pay him any attention.

Once Belle had finished sniffing, Kate led the way. It turned out her flat was on the same route he'd explored earlier. The enormous pine tree he'd passed in daylight was transformed into a twinkling, golden Christmas tree.

'Now that's what I call a tree,' he said in awe.

Kate laughed. 'It is rather wonderful.'

A few minutes later, they said goodnight at her door. Jack felt in a daze as he walked home, shocked how his life had transformed in just 48 hours.

***

The next morning, Christmas Eve, Jack kept checking his phone for a text from Kate to confirm Grace was being discharged, but nothing came through.

He kept busy cleaning the house and even went shopping to stock the fridge and buy some of the festive goodies he knew Grace liked. Surely, they'd let her home for Christmas.

Belle seemed to sense his restless mood and paced the room.

'What should we do?'

The dog stopped and stared at him, tilting her head sideways. He realised her white mane was looking matted. 'Maybe a groom?'

He'd seen the grooming brushes in a basket in the front room next to Grace's knitting supplies.

'I've come this far, Belle. We can do this, can't we?'

She saw the brush and sat dutifully still while he worked the knots from her fur. It took over an hour, but felt strangely therapeutic.

Jack found a bow and put her fur in a cute top knot. 'I have to say that you are a most beautiful dog.'

Belle licked his hand, her tongue unexpectedly soft and warm. He laughed, feeling as though it was her way of accepting him.

Jack was just thinking of calling the hospital for news when he heard a vehicle pull up outside. He and Belle rushed to the front room window to see the hospital transport opening its back doors.

'About time, hey girl.' He patted Belle on the head as she stood with her paws on the windowsill, watching all the activity.

It took a while, but eventually Grace was wheeled up to the front door. They'd provided her with a zimmer frame. She used it to walk, limping, but unaided, into the house.

'Where's my baby?' were her first words.

The concern knitting her brow dissolved as Belle gave a responding bark and then whimpered impatiently from where Jack had temporarily locked her in the front room.

'I didn't want her to knock you off your feet and send you straight back into the hospital,' he joked. 'Are you ready?'

'Of course I am.'

Jack let Belle loose but was ready to assist if Grace looked unsteady.

The dog wagged and wiggled in circles around them, and she licked Grace's hands and face when she bent for a big cuddle.

His neighbour was openly crying, while Jack watched their reunion through watering eyes.

'I missed you so much,' Grace said, and Belle barked in agreement.

'Look at my beautiful girl. Jack's done such a good job with you.' She wiped away tears as she met his gaze. All the thanks he needed showed in her grateful smile.

Gus arrived next and wrapped himself around his owner's legs. Grace swept him up into her arms, despite his size, and kissed his head. Her rewards were headbutts and purrs.

'Thank you so much for looking after my babies.'

'Any time,' he said gruffly, and coughed to clear emotion from his throat. 'It's good to see you home.'

He helped her manoeuvre her zimmer frame into the front room, where she gasped at the flashing Christmas tree he'd switched on before he answered the door. 'You have made an old woman very happy, Jack.'

While Grace settled into her favourite armchair, he went to make them a cup of tea. Belle remained at her owner's side, looking adoringly up at her.

As he returned with drinks and a box of shortbread, Kate turned up, and there were more tearful hugs.

'You two have done a wonderful job here. Thank you so much,' Grace said. She sank back into the chair and sipped her tea, looking frail but happy with a blanket over her knees and Belle resting at her feet. 'I'm so lucky to have such good friends looking out for me.'

'It's been no trouble at all,' Jack said, and Kate murmured agreement.

She pointed Kate to the sideboard. 'Could you pass me the carrier bag from the cupboard, please?'

Grace took the bag from her and removed two silver wrapped parcels. 'I know it's early, but I wanted to give you these now.'

She handed them each a present with a festive name tag and a big red ribbon. Jack sat holding it on his lap.

'Open them, please.'

Reminded of being a child at Christmas time, Jack tore off the paper. Inside was a beautifully knitted jumper in pine-tree green and made of the softest wool.

'It's gorgeous, Grace, thank you.' Kate held her dusky-red knitted jumper up to her cheek and rubbed the soft fibres against her skin. It complimented her deep auburn hair and warm brown eyes.

'I hope you'll wear them tomorrow when you come here for Christmas dinner. If you're both free to join me, that is?'

They looked at each other. 'Yes,' they said together.

Grace's face broke into a wide grin. 'It will be a lovely day with my two favourite people, and my two fur babies.'

Seeing the joy light up Grace and Kate's faces, Jack realised for the first time in years, he was looking forward to Christmas day too.

Dear Reader

I hope you've enjoyed my latest collection of short stories in the Winter Warmer Series. Please consider leaving a review and telling your friends about my books. Every review can help new readers discover my work and it's a wonderful way to support an author.

If you want to get in touch, please use the contact form on my website;

www.suzannerogersonfantasyauthor.com.

You can also keep up to date with new publications by joining my newsletter (links on the website) or by following my author page on Amazon.

If you liked this collection of short stories, A Christmas Wish is also available in the Winter Warmer Series.

Also by the Author

Short Story Anthologies

Fantasy Short Stories
(featuring characters from Visions of Zarua &
Silent Sea Chronicles)
Love, Loss and Life In Between

Winter Warmers Short Story Series
A Christmas Wish
A Little Christmas Magic

Romance Books

The Mermaid Hotel Series
COMING SOON

Fantasy Books

Silent Sea Chronicles Trilogy
The Lost Sentinel - Book 1
The Sentinel's Reign - Book 2
The Sentinel's Alliance - Book 3
Also available as Silent Sea Chronicles Boxset

Standalone Epic Fantasy
Visions of Zarua - Also available in audiobook

Acknowledgements

Thank you to the family who have supported my writing dream. You know who you are.
And thanks to my library group beta readers for your critiques and encouragement.

About the Author

Suzanne lives in Middlesex, England with her husband, two children, a crazy spaniel and a demanding cat. Her writing journey began at the age of twelve when she completed her first novel. Giving up work to raise a family gave Suzanne the impetus to take her attempts at novel writing beyond the first draft, and she is lucky enough to have a husband who supports her dream - even if he does occasionally hint that she might think about getting a proper job one day.

She loves gardening and has a Hebe (shrub) fetish. She enjoys cooking with ingredients from the garden and regularly feeds unsuspecting guests vegetable-based cakes. Suzanne collects books, is interested in history and enjoys wandering around castles and old ruins whilst being immersed in the past. Most of all, she loves to escape with a great film, binge watch TV shows, or soak in a hot bubble bath with an ice cream and a book.

Find Suzanne on her website for information about new releases and follow the link to join her mailing list. www.suzannerogersonfantasyauthor.com
X @rogersonsm
Instagram @suzannemrogerson
Facebook @suzannerogersonfantasyauthor

Printed in Great Britain
by Amazon